ALLAN AHLBERG

Fast Fox Goes Crazy

Illustrated by
ANDRÉ AMSTUTZ

VIKING • PUFFIN

VIKING/PUFFIN
Published by the Penguin Group: London, New York, Australia, Canada and New Zealand
Penguin Books Ltd, Registered Offices: Harmondsworth, Middlesex, England

First published by Viking 1999
1 3 5 7 9 10 8 6 4 2
Published in Puffin Books 1999
1 3 5 7 9 10 8 6 4 2

Printed in Singapore by Imago Publishing Ltd

A CIP catalogue record for this book is available from the British Library
ISBN 0–670–87994–0 Hardback
ISBN 0–140–56400–4 Paperback

Fast Fox is counting chickens.
One chicken,
two chickens,
three chickens.

Fast fox is happy.
Three chickens – yes, yes, yes!
He picks up his sack.

But then – what's this?
Four chickens,
five chickens,
six chickens!

Fast Fox is very happy.
Six chickens –
Yes, yes, yes, yes, yes, yes!
He opens his sack.

But then – *more* chickens.
Seven chickens,
eight chickens,
nine chickens . . .

ten chickens!

Fast Fox goes crazy.
Ten chickens – Yes!

Yes!

Yes!

Yes!

Yes–Yes–Yes–Yes!

YES!

YES!

And off he runs
to find a bigger sack.

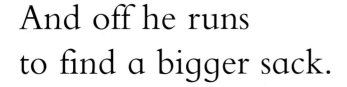

Meanwhile . . .
the chickens are having a party.
All their friends have come.
Mother Hen is in the kitchen.

Slow Dog helps . . . slowly . . . with the fun and games.

The chickens play
hide-and-seek.
Fast Fox watches.

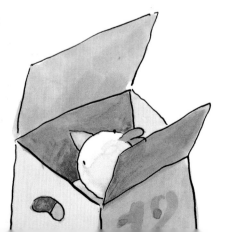

The chickens play
Blind man's buff.
Fast Fox waits.

The chickens play
running – and jumping –
and bouncing
on the great big . . .
bouncy castle.

Fast Fox *opens his sack.*

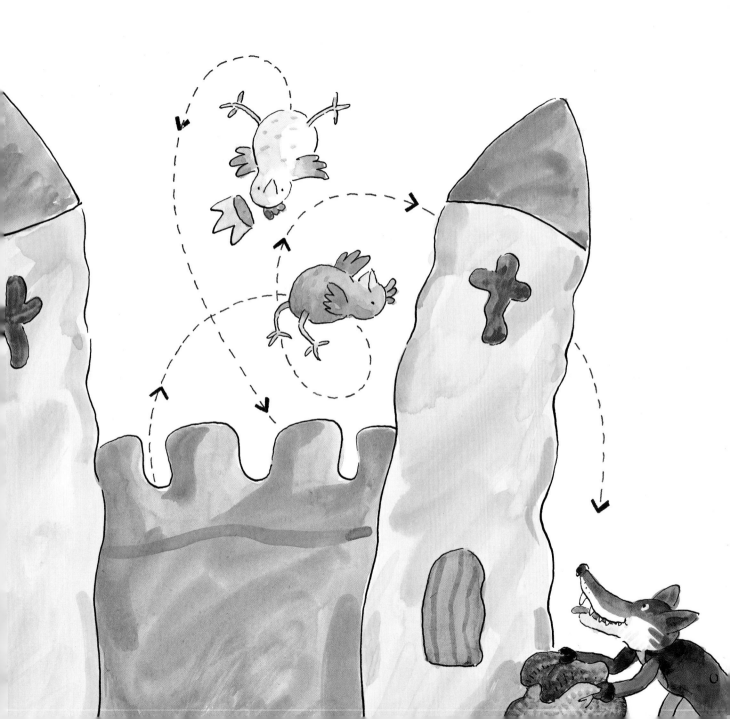

One, two, three,
the chickens run.
Four, five, six,
the chickens jump.
Seven, eight, nine,
the chickens bounce . . .

into the sack.

Fast Fox goes crazy again.
Nine chickens — Yes—

Yes – yes – yes – yes – yes – yes – yes –yes!

One more to go.

Meanwhile . . .
the last little chicken is worried.
"I cannot bounce," she says.
"It is too scary."

"Not . . . to . . . worry,"
Slow Dog says.
"It's easy.
Watch . . . me."

Slow Dog jumps
and bounces – Whee! –

and lands.

So the story ends.
The chickens have their party.
Mother Hen dozes.

Slow Dog helps . . . slowly . . . with the washing up.

Meanwhile . . .
back in his house –
"Ninety-eight chickens!"
Fast Fox is still counting –
"Ninety-nine chickens!"
and going crazy . . .
"*A hundred chickens!*"

. . . in his dreams.

The End

THE FAST FOX, SLOW DOG BOOKS

If you liked this story,
why not read three more?
Try

Chicken, Chips and Peas
Slow Dog Falling
The Hen House

Fast Fox is always hungry.
Slow Dog is always sleepy.
Mother Hen is always on the phone . . .
and her chickens are *always* in trouble!

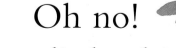

Oh no!
Those poor little chickens . . .

. . . who can save them?